BILL PICKETT

by Rozanne Lanczak Williams
illustrated by Suzanne Muse

Harcourt

Orlando   Boston   Dallas   Chicago   San Diego

Visit *The Learning Site!*

www.harcourtschool.com

"Bill Picket was the greatest sweat-and-dirt cowhand that ever lived—bar none."

—Zack Miller, owner of the 101 Ranch

Ole' Bill Pickett was a rodeo man.
No better cowboy could be found.
He was rough, he was tough,
And he couldn't get enough
Of wrestlin' those wild critters
to the ground.

**Bill Pickett was born
and raised in Texas.**

*Born on a farm down Texas way,
Bill was the second of thirteen.
While others played and did their chores,
Bill would wander off and dream.*

3

He'd wave to the cowboys on the dusty trail
And join in singin' a song.

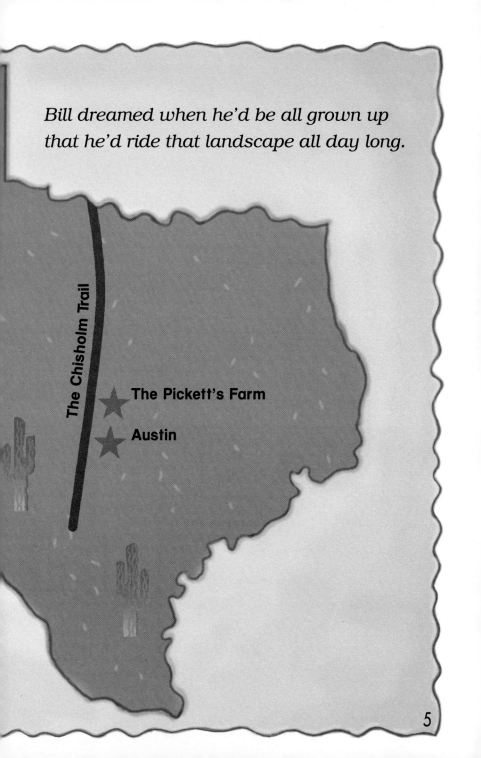

Bill dreamed when he'd be all grown up
that he'd ride that landscape all day long.

The Chisholm Trail

The Pickett's Farm

Austin

At fifteen, Bill left home, leavin' his kin behind.
Sitting on a dappled horse, that Bill was one of a kind.

Bill learned to ride and rope like the best,
Like the cowboys he waved to on the trail.
"Thatta boy, Bill. Show that hoss who's
the boss!"
Yelled the cowhands sittin' on the rail.

One day on the ranch, a mean steer took off.
No cowboy could bring the dogie back.
Wild Bill took off—riding like the wind
And he jumped on that critter's neck.

Bill held tight, he wouldn't let go.
He grabbed that steer by the horns.
Next thing you know, Bill bit its lip!
And the stunt of bulldogging was born.

In not much time, the word got around.
Bill gave many an exhibition of his skill.
He signed up with a show—a rodeo!
The crowd yelled, "Bring on that Bull-doggin' Bill!"

A big-time rancher cornered Bill one day:
"Here's a business deal for you.
Bring your family to my ranch an' join
my show.
You'll be a star before you're through!"

101 Ranch and Wild West Show

Thousands of people all
over the world
Came to see Bill's bull-
doggin' act.
No one could bring down
a bull like Bill.
"He's the best," said his
boss. "That's a fact!"

Some say the rodeo stunt of bulldogging was invented by Bill. His act was amazing. He would ride alongside a steer and jump on its back. Then he would turn its head around until he could bite the cow's lip. This would bring the steer down.

Bill Pickett is one of the best-known rodeo cowboys who ever lived. He was the first black cowboy to be inducted into the Rodeo Hall of Fame.

Bill Pickett was featured on a U.S. postage stamp. His stamp was popular with those people who collect stamps.

Bill Pickett 1870–1932

Ole' Bill Pickett was a rodeo man.
No better cowboy could be found.
He was rough and he couldn't get enough
Of wrestlin' those wild critters to the ground.